THIS WALKER BOOK BELONGS TO:

_____

_____ _____

_____

_____

For Bryan and Sarah

with thanks to
Melissa Appleton, Sarah and Rowan Dale
for the elephant endpapers, and David Lloyd
for seeing the wood.

First published 1991
by Walker Books Ltd, 87 Vauxhall Walk
London SE11 5HJ

© 1991 Penny Dale

This edition published 1993

4 6 8 10 9 7 5 3

Printed in Hong Kong/China

British Library Cataloguing in Publication Data
A catalogue record for this book is
available from the British Library.

ISBN 0-7445-3071-7

The Elephant Tree

Penny Dale

WALKER BOOKS

AND SUBSIDIARIES

LONDON • BOSTON • SYDNEY

Elephant wanted to climb a tree.

So we went to find the elephant tree.

We walked and we walked.

We looked and we looked.

"Is this the elephant tree?"
"No," said the birds.
"It's the bird tree."

"Is this the elephant tree?"

"No," said the monkeys.
"It's the monkey tree."

"Is this the elephant tree?"
"No," said the tigers.
"It's the tiger tree."

"Are any of these the
elephant tree?"

"No," said the bears.

"These are bear trees."

We ran and we ran.

We walked and we walked.

We looked and we looked.

But we still couldn't find the elephant tree.

Never mind, Elephant.

Wait and see.

Here it is. Look.

The elephant tree.

MORE WALKER PAPERBACKS
For You to Enjoy

Also by Penny Dale

ROSIE'S BABIES
written by Martin Waddell

Winner of the Best Book for Babies Award and Shortlisted for the Kate Greenaway Medal.

"Deals with sibling jealousy in a very convincing way."
Child Education

0-7445-2335-4   £4.99

BET YOU CAN'T!

"A lively argumentative dialogue – using simple, repetitive words – between two children.
Illustrated with great humour and realism."
Practical Parenting

0-7445-1225-5   £4.50

WAKE UP, MR B!

A small girl plays some imaginative early morning
games with her dog.

"Perceptive, domestic illustrations fill a varied cartoon-strip format …
making this a lovely tell-it-yourself picture book."
The Good Book Guide

0-7445-1467-3   £4.99

TEN IN THE BED

"A subtle variation on the traditional nursery song, illustrated with
wonderfully warm pictures … crammed with amusing details."
Practical Parenting

0-7445-1340-5   £4.99

Walker Paperbacks are available from most booksellers, or by post from B.B.C.S., P.O. Box 941, Hull, North Humberside HU1 3YQ
24 hour telephone credit card line 01482 224626

To order, send: Title, author, ISBN number and price for each book ordered, your full name and address,
cheque or postal order payable to BBCS for the total amount and allow the following for postage and packing:
UK and BFPO: £1.00 for the first book, and 50p for each additional book to a maximum of £3.50.
Overseas and Eire: £2.00 for the first book, £1.00 for the second and 50p for each additional book.

Prices and availability are subject to change without notice.